Janina Domanska is the well-known artist who illustrated THE COCONUT THIEVES, which was selected by *Book Week* as a Prize Book in the 1964 Children's Spring Book Festival. She has also illustrated such favorites as Dorothy Kunhardt's GAS STATION GUS, Natalie Savage Carlson's THE SONG OF THE LOP-EARED MULE, and MORE TALES OF FARAWAY FOLK by Babette Deutsch and Avrahm Yarmolinsky.

In addition to her work in children's book illustration, she has had several gallery exhibitions of her painting, and many of her illustrations have appeared in such magazines as *Harper's* and *The Reporter*. WHY SO MUCH NOISE? is the first book for which she has done both the words and pictures.

Janina Domanska was born in Warsaw, Poland, and now makes her home in Valley Stream, New York, with her husband, a journalist and playwright.

Many years ago in ancient India the Elephant and his friend the Tiger played a game to see who could make a noisy monkey fall down from a tree. "If you make him fall," said the cunning Tiger, "you can eat me. But if I make him fall, I will eat you." And the Tiger won.

"I will give you seven days," he said to the Elephant. "And then I will eat you." All week long the Elephant wailed. "Why so much noise?" the animals asked. Finally, the little Mouse Deer came to see what he could do to help.

How the tiny Mouse Deer tricked the Tiger and saved the Elephant's life makes this folktale one to be treasured by all children. Janina Domanska's pictures are as full of vitality and mirth as the story.

WHY SO MUCH NOISE?

why so much noise?

RETOLD AND ILLUSTRATED BY
JANINA DOMANSKA

HARPER & ROW, PUBLISHERS
NEW YORK

This story is an adaptation of the tale entitled
"The Elephant Has a Bet With the Tiger,"
by Walter William Skeat.

TO SUSAN CARR

Many years ago in ancient India, the Elephant said to his friend the Tiger, "That long-tailed monkey up there in the trees is making so much noise, we can hardly hear ourselves talk. Let's see if we can scare him so much that he will fall down and go away."

Because he was always hungry, the cunning old Tiger said, "Let's play a game. If you make him fall down, you can eat me. But if I make him fall, I will eat you."

"Very well," replied the Elephant, laughing and flapping his big ears.

"You go first," said the Tiger.

The Elephant took a deep breath.
"*Au...Au...Au...*" he trumpeted.

The earth trembled and the trees shook, but the monkey did not fall. Finally the Elephant gave up. "You try," he said to the Tiger. "I have no breath left."

The Tiger hunched his back and let out a tremendous roar. The monkey fell at his feet.

"So!" exclaimed the Tiger to the Elephant. "Do I eat you now?"

"Oh, please, not now!" sobbed the Elephant. "Let me go home and say good-bye to my wife and children."

The Tiger nodded. "I will give you seven days, my friend. And then I will eat you."

The Elephant thanked him and set off through the forest, weeping and bellowing.

After telling his family the bad news, the Elephant and his wife and children spent the seven days wailing so loudly that none of the other animals could sleep.

"Why so much noise?" they asked one another. But no one could answer.

Finally the little Mouse Deer came to the Elephant's house. "What has happened, my friend?" he asked. "We hear you bellowing every day and every night. It's bad enough having to listen to the rain, without you and your family making all this noise."

The unhappy Elephant sobbed out his story, and the Mouse Deer laughed.

"Don't worry," he said. "That old Tiger is not going to eat you. I won't let him."

"You won't?" asked the Elephant. "Oh, my friend, if you save my life, my family and I will be grateful to you forever."

The Mouse Deer told the Elephant to get a jar of molasses and bring it to him at once.

The Elephant went to look for the molasses at the house of a sugarcane farmer.

The man was so frightened that he ran and hid in the fields.

The Elephant found the molasses and quickly returned, with the jar, to the Mouse Deer.

"Well done," exclaimed the Mouse Deer. "The seven days are up tomorrow. We will approach the Tiger together.

But before we leave, ask your wife to pour the molasses all over your back."

The Elephant did as he was told.

The next morning he arrived at the Mouse Deer's house, covered with the sweet, sticky molasses.

"Splendid!" cried the Mouse Deer. "Now let's go and scare that old Tiger. I am going to jump on your back. When I start licking the molasses, bellow as loud as you can and pretend you are being eaten alive."

The Elephant made so much noise as the Mouse Deer licked the sweet stuff that the Tiger came bounding out of the jungle to see what was happening.

As soon as the Mouse Deer saw the Tiger he shouted, "You are not such good eating, old Elephant. If I could only catch a big fat tiger, I would get a real meal!"

The Tiger heard and was terrified.

He turned around and ran crashing through the jungle until he met the Old Ape.

"Why are you running so fast, Friend Tiger?" asked the Ape. "And why so much noise, just now when the rains are upon us?"

"What do you mean, so much noise?" replied the Tiger. "There is a Thing eating Friend Elephant alive, and he wants to eat me too. I heard him say so."

"Who was he?" asked the Old Ape.

"I don't know," replied the Tiger. "But he was very fierce and had a loud, high voice."

"Hmmm. I wonder if it could have been Friend Mouse Deer," said the Old Ape.

"Of course not!" the Tiger cried. "How could Friend Mouse Deer possibly eat me? Why, I could swallow him in one bite! And anyway, he eats only fruits and leaves—not elephants and tigers!"

"Oh," said the Old Ape. "Well, let's go back and see what is going on."

They raced back to where the Elephant was still screaming and bellowing.

As soon as the Mouse Deer caught sight of them he stopped licking the molasses and cried, "Hi, Old Ape! What kind of a trick are you playing on me? You promised to bring me two tigers. One is no good. I am hungry. Now go and get the other one—quick!"

The Tiger turned and fled back into the jungle with the Ape at his heels.

When they were at a safe distance, the Tiger snarled at the Ape. Baring his sharp teeth, he said, "A fine friend you are—trying to trick me."

"No, no," cried the Ape. "That dreadful Thing—"

"Quiet!" roared the Tiger. I know what you had planned. I have a good mind to eat you right here and now."

But the Ape was too quick. Before the Tiger could spring, he was high up in a tree. The Tiger paced around in circles, lashing his tail. "You are right to stay up there, Old Ape," he called. "If I ever catch you on the ground, I will eat you —just as that terrible Thing ate poor Friend Elephant."

That is why the Tiger and the Ape are still enemies, but the Elephant and the clever little Mouse Deer are close friends.

Any animal in the jungle will tell you that.

DATE DUE

NO 17 67	MAR 2 1 '80	APR 1 5 1991	
JA 26 '68			
FE 23 '68			
AP 19 '68			
DE 6 '68			
AP 25 '69			
RETURNED			
JA 25 70			
MR 20 '70		WITHDRAWN FROM	
70		OHIO NORTHERN	
RETURNED		UNIVERSITY LIBRARY	
ENCLOSED			
RETURNED DE 3 70			
RETURNED 71			
RETURNED AUG 2 5 1972			

GAYLORD   PRINTED IN U.S.A.